DOCTOR · WHO

DECIDE YOUR
DESTINY

BBC CHILDREN'S BOOKS
Published by the Penguin Group
Penguin Books Ltd, 80 Strand, London, WC2R 0RL, England
Penguin Group (USA) Inc., 375 Hudson Street, New York, New York 10014, USA
Penguin Books (Australia) Ltd, 250 Camberwell Road, Camberwell, Victoria 3124, Australia
(A division of Pearson Australia Group Pty Ltd)
Canada, India, New Zealand, South Africa
Published by BBC Children's Books, 2008
This edition produced for The Book People Ltd, Hall Wood Avenue, Haydock, St Helens. WA11 9UL.
Text and design © Children's Character Books, 2008
Written by Colin Brake
10 9 8 7 6 5 4 3 2 1
ISBN-13: 978-1-85613-148-3
ISBN-10: 1-85613-148-3
Printed in Great Britain by Clays Ltd, St Ives plc

DOCTOR·WHO

DECIDE YOUR DESTINY

Lost Luggage

by Colin Brake

Lost Luggage

1 | The blue box looked like a good place to hide from your mates but you had no idea that entering the box would lead you to meet an alien named the Doctor.

You look around the vast chamber you've stumbled into, trying to make sense of it. In the centre of the room a many-sided control console stands on a raised platform. Vine-like power cables hang from the ceiling and you notice that the walls curve in, between organic-looking coral supports.

'But it was just a blue box,' you whisper, with the familiar feeling of awe you always get when you go into a church or a temple.

'It's dimensionally transcendental,' the Doctor tells you, 'bigger on the inside,' he adds helpfully.

The Doctor introduces himself and explains that you've stumbled into his space/time machine — the TARDIS. You tell him that you need to get back to your friends and his expression turns serious.

'I'm afraid that you wandered in just as I completed setting the controls. We'll have to wait until we land before I can put the old girl into reverse,' he tells you.

'How long will that take?' you ask, worried.

Just then the engine sounds die away with a dull thump.

'Not long at all,' the Doctor grins, quickly checking the instruments on the console.

'Where are we?' you wonder. 'And when?'

The Doctor shoots you a quick look. 'Oh, I do like a curious mind! Shall we have a quick peek? Just a little look, and then I'll get you home…'

You can see that he is really eager to explore and you find that his enthusiasm is infectious.

'Okay then,' you tell him, smiling.

If the Doctor leads the way out, go to 11. If he lets you exit first, go to 32.

2 You run back into the matter transmitter room and find the Doctor sitting on the floor looking a little bemused.

'Collywobbles.' he repeats, 'What an odd word that is. Haven't used it before, won't use it again. Well, maybe one more time. Did that give you the collywobbles too?'

You tell him that you don't know what he's talking about but agree that it was a very strange sensation.

The Doctor gets to his feet and you show him the way to the corridor. He immediately points at the space freighter you saw arriving a minute ago. 'That's the *Hulke*,' he tells you.

'So that's where the TARDIS is?' you say, with a great deal of relief. 'But how are we going to get over there — it's miles away?' you wonder.

If the Doctor finds an electronic car, go to 7. If you set off on foot, go to 41.

3 The Doctor explains you are on a Space Beacon.

'Is that something different to StarBase Gamma?' you ask.

The Doctor nods, grimly.

'StarBase Gamma is a major spaceport — this is just a tiny Space Service Station,' he explains. 'Our ship must have made an unscheduled stop.'

'I guess we just have to wait until the next ship comes by,' you suggest.

The Doctor tells you that this Space Beacon has a limited air supply — it's not designed to house humans.

The minutes begin to drag as you try to conserve your oxygen. You start to find it hard to breathe. Your eyelids are getting heavy. It's hard to keep your eyes open.

Finally as the world begins to fade to black you faintly hear a loud clang.

If you come round inside a spaceship, go to 33. If you come round still on the Beacon, go to 70.

4 The doors suddenly open and thick black smoke bellows out. A figure emerges, coughing and stumbling. It is the junior engineer.

You ask him if the Doctor is alright but he can't answer for coughing. Not daring to wait for more information you grab the fire extinguisher and prepare to run into the room.

'Wait!' It's the medic. She passes you a wet cloth. 'Hold this over your mouth and nose,' she instructs you, 'and keep down close to the floor.'

You thank her and enter the room, bent almost double.

Inside the room the smoke is even thicker but, like the medic suggested, it's thinner nearer the floor. You manage to make out the Doctor's trainers, still standing near the console. Somehow he is still on his feet.

If you get the fire extinguisher to the Doctor, go to 13. If you start using the fire extinguisher, go to 35.

5 The outer door begins to open again and the air inside the airlock begins to escape.

'The tube's disconnected,' the Doctor tells you, horrified. Quickly he produces the sonic screwdriver and aims it at the control box. To your relief the door quickly reverses its motion and shuts again with a firm clunk. The Doctor presses another control on the screwdriver and informs you that he has deadlocked the door for maximum safety.

'I think we lost quite a bit of oxygen,' you reply, gasping for breath, 'the air in here is rather thin.'

'Then we'd better get into the main part of this ship,' comments the Doctor.

The Doctor presses an intercom button. 'Hello,' he says, 'is anyone there?' By way of an answer the inner door begins to open.

If someone is waiting for you, go to 99.
If the corridor beyond the door is empty,
go to 89.

6 It's Dave, the cleaner you met in the Hub. He quickly explains that he is in fact an undercover customs officer named Nikesh, working to try and secure a conviction against Hawkeye Pete's gang.

'Unfortunately my cover got blown,' he confesses, 'and they threw me in here.'

The Doctor comes up with a plan. He tells the pirates that he is the senior customs officer on the case and he knows where the StarFire can be found. He describes the TARDIS and explains that it is a safe with biological locks that can only be opened by all three of you.

The pirates fall for the yarn the Doctor spins and take you to the TARDIS.

When the Doctor opens the door, Hawkeye Pete steps forward.

If you all squeeze in before the pirate can, go to 43. If the pirate leader gets into the TARDIS, go to 75.

The Doctor has moved further back along the corridor and discovers an alcove containing a small electric vehicle. He calls you over. The car looks a bit like a golf buggy. Using his trusty sonic screwdriver, the Doctor gets the engine to start and soon you are speeding along at about ten miles an hour. The Doctor grins at you.

'Okay so it's still going to take a while but it's better than walking,' he says.

Soon you reach the end of the corridor and emerge into the main part of the Space Station. This area is more populated and the Doctor has to weave in and out of a great deal of traffic. Many of the vehicles are driven by robots but there are also a large number of humans and humanoid aliens as well.

It's a bit like driving through a major city in the rush hour but the Doctor proves to be a skilful driver and you soon reach a quieter stretch of 'road' that takes you to the unloading area for the freighter.

The Doctor parks the car you 'borrowed' and suggests that you both look for someone in charge.

The Doctor stops an official-looking man in a dark suit and asks him if he can help you locate your lost property.

'Lost property? On the *Hulke*? I don't think so!' answers the man.

'But we lost something at the Hub. We were told it was on this ship,' you explain.

'Everything on that ship is accounted for,' explains the man. 'Check the manifest if you don't believe me.'

He passes a hand-held computer to the Doctor who scans through pages of data as fast as the screen can display them.

If there is no mention of any lost luggage on-board, go to 18. If the lost luggage has been moved to another ship, go to 71.

'Ten thousand kilometres!' you exclaim, repeating what the Doctor has told you. 'How are we ever going to find anything in a Space Station that size? It could take years!'

'Or more,' agrees the Doctor, 'if you were just wandering up and down aimlessly. But we won't be...' From one of his coat pockets the Doctor produces something that looks like...

'A mobile phone?'

The Doctor shakes his head. 'A TARDIS detector. Well, to be precise it's an artron energy detector but it amounts to the same thing.' He flicks open the device and it begins flashing in a slow rhythm.

'As we get warmer the flashing will speed up,' the Doctor tells you, setting off at such a high pace, you have to run to keep up.

If the signal leads you to take the lift up, go to 60. If the signal leads you to take the lift down, go to 54.

'Excuse me,' you say again, in a louder tone.

The man turns and you can now see that he is wearing big spongy ear plugs which he removes.

'Sorry, kid, gets a bit noisy down here,' he tells you with a smile. 'What can I do for you?'

Prompted by the Doctor's voice in your ear, you tell the man that you lost a blue box on the Hub and that you believe it is on the *Hulke*.

'You need to try the security chief,' the man suggests, 'his office is on level 2.'

'We're on our way now,' mutters the Doctor in your ear, but then his voice is cut off by a massive explosion.

The helpful man is pointing towards a lift. 'That's the one you need,' he tells you.

If the lift is working, go to 73. If the lift isn't working, go to 38.

10 The corridor outside the matter transport room is completely empty but the view is stunning, as a window the length of the corridor allows you to see the rest of the Space Station.

To call it a Space Station seems an understatement. StarBase Gamma is like a city in orbit, a mass of skyscraper-like structures emerging from a central core.

The scale of it is difficult to take in but you see a tiny spacecraft docking at the end of one arm and are shocked to realise that it is, in fact, a huge space freighter and that you are looking it at from a distance of some miles.

You hear a noise from behind you and a familiar voice.

'Oh now that gave me the collywobbles!'

If you followed the Doctor into the police matter transporter, go to 88. If you went first into the police matter transporter, go to 2.

11 You follow the Doctor out through the doors and discover that the TARDIS has landed on a glass-encased bridge. Below, you can see a vast football pitch-sized hall which is filled with hundreds of desks and queues of people, bags and cases of luggage on hovering trolleys, and a loud buzz of a thousand conversations in as many different languages.

'It looks like an airport or something,' you observe.

'Nothing gets past you, does it!' comments the Doctor, with a grin. 'Actually this is a spaceport — in fact, the biggest in this sector of space. We're somewhere in the late twenty-fifth century and this,' he waves a hand in the direction of the whole area, 'is the Hub.'

'Excuse me?' says someone behind you.

If the speaker is a member of the spaceport ground crew, go to 52. If the speaker is a fellow traveller, go to 69.

Emergency lighting comes on inside the cabin where you are sitting, throwing a spooky red light over everything.

'What's happening?' you ask the Doctor.

He is already making his way to the bulkhead door. 'Power loss,' he answers you, over his shoulder, as he wrenches the door open.

The Doctor leads the way out of the passenger cabin into the private areas of the spacecraft. With an unerring sense of direction he soon finds his way to the engine room. It's a large chamber full of technology, centred on a thick column from which dense black smoke is pouring.

A balding, middle-aged man dressed in red overalls labelled 'ENGINEERING' in white letters lies injured on the floor, where a medical officer is attending to him. Elsewhere in the room a young man with untidy blond hair, in similar red overalls, is looking at various computer read-outs with a look of panic.

'What's the problem?' the Doctor asks him.

'Unstable fuel in the fusion chamber,' the young engineer looks completely petrified, 'and I'm worried the whole thing is going to explode.'

'That doesn't seem like something we want to be seeing, does it?' mutters the Doctor, taking the young man's place at the control consoles.

'Can you fix it?' you ask the Doctor.

Without taking his eyes from the read-outs the Doctor assures you that he can sort the problem out. 'The question is, can I do it in time?'

The Doctor's hands are a blur as he makes quick adjustments to various controls.

'Can you see a fire extinguisher?' he asks you.

You cast your eyes around the chamber looking for something that might be a fire extinguisher.

If you see a cylinder handing on the wall, go to 31. If you can't see anything, go to 26.

13 The Doctor grabs the extinguisher and begins to operate it. To your surprise, rather than spraying a foam or gas on to the flames, it seems to act in the opposite fashion — sucking all the smoke out of the air and extinguishing the flames at the same time. In a matter of seconds the fire and smoke have all but disappeared.

The Doctor gives you a grin. 'Anti-fire,' he tells you, in a rather unhelpful way, 'thanks for your help.'

Now the fire has gone the Doctor can turn his attention back to the engine trouble. He flicks a couple of switches and then steps back. The engine noise, which has been an ugly roar, drops back to a gentle hum.

The crew are also grateful for the assistance in the crisis and when you get back to your seats they bring you a wonderful meal. After you've eaten you realise how tired all the excitement has made you and fall into a deep sleep.

Some time later the Doctor wakes you up and tells you that it's time to get off the ship.

Saying goodbye to the grateful crew, you step out of the airlock and find yourselves in a rather spartan Space Station.

'I thought we were going to Saturn?' you mention to the Doctor.

He agrees, 'So did I!' He quickly uses his sonic screwdriver to gain access to the Space Station's computers.

'This is an automated service station — a refuelling stop. We've managed to get ahead of the ship carrying the TARDIS. It should reach here soon,' he announces.

You settle down to wait. Finally, after what seems like an age, the ship you are waiting for appears on the screen.

If the ship docks, go to 37. If the ship fails to stop, go to 61.

14 Alarms begin to sound and emergency red lighting comes into effect. Seconds later the reason for this becomes clear as a huge shockwave knocks you from your feet.

'The ship's under attack,' explains the Doctor.

Commander Jacoby orders his pilot to take evasive action. Then he summons a junior officer and waves in your direction.

'Get these people to the emergency transmat station,' he commands, 'and beam them to a place of safety. Are we in range of the Space Base?'

The junior officer nods and leads you away.

The matter transmitter station is located behind the bridge and consists of a sending platform and a control desk situated behind a thick plastic shield which you look at curiously.

'Don't ask,' suggests the Doctor as you are both placed in position.

If the Doctor is sent first, go to 55. If you go first, go to 29.

You walk into the unloading area of StarBase Gamma, trying to look as much like an innocent tourist as you can. A tiny earpiece connects you to the Doctor and it gives you comfort to hear his encouraging tones as you wander between the large robots that are unloading the container pods from the ship.

Although you cannot see anything that looks like a camera you know that multiple images of you, from various angles, will be appearing on a bank of TV screens in front of the Doctor.

Amongst the automated unloading robots there are a number of living stevedores, both human and alien. You see a human in dirty grey overalls and wander over to him.

'Excuse me,' you begin, 'but I seem to have lost something of mine, can you help me?'

If he answers you, go to 81. If he ignores you, go to 9.

16 You find it difficult to walk forward as the springy surface of the tube wobbles under your feet.

'It's designed for low gravity situations,' explains the Doctor, from behind you, as you fall.

He helps you to your feet and shows you a handrail running along the length of the tube, which you can use to support your progress.

With the aid of this you are soon able to get to the end of the tube and find yourself stepping into another airlock. The Doctor joins you and shuts the outer door.

'Right, let's find out what kind of ship this is,' suggests the Doctor and tries to operate the inner door. He frowns.

'That's odd,' he tells you, 'this has been deadbolt locked. Someone doesn't like hitchhikers.'

If the airlock begins to fill with gas, go to 64. If the outer door of the airlock begins to open again, go to 5.

17 | You follow the Doctor into a standard-looking airlock and watch as he closes the outer door. A peculiar purple light passes over you slowly and a hum fills the air.

'What's happening?' you ask the Doctor.

'Cleansing scan,' he tells you, 'making sure we're not bringing any nasty micro-organisms on-board. Standard operating procedure these days. Wasn't always the case, mind you, I once landed on a ship with an Earth girl who had a cold and nearly wiped out an entire race.'

The scan concludes and normal lighting comes back on.

'Now what?' you wonder.

The Doctor looks towards the inner doors.

'With a bit of luck those doors will open and we can try and find the TARDIS,' he answers, hopefully. Luck must be on your side as the doors begin to open.

**If someone is waiting for you, go to 99.
If the corridor beyond the door is empty, go to 89.**

18 The Doctor takes you to one side as a huge robot rumbles past you.

'I don't understand,' you complain, 'the TARDIS was meant to be on the *Hulke*, that's what we were told.'

The Doctor nods. 'Looks like we weren't told the truth,' he comments, checking a small electronic device that he has fished out of his pocket. 'No artron energy trace confirms it. We've been on a wild goose chase. Right then — back to the hub. Do not pass go. Do not collect two hundred pounds...'

The Doctor leads you back into the main area of the Base and finds a travel agent. You're in luck — there is a ship leaving in the next few minutes, which is scheduled to reach the Hub in a matter of hours.

If you can get on the Express flight, go to 42. If there is only one seat available, go to 79.

The storeroom you've been told the TARDIS is in is more like a warehouse — it's huge!

'This could take forever!' you comment, looking at the sight before you.

In front of you are countless rows of floor to ceiling storage compartments, enough to fill a room that is easily the size of Wembley Stadium. The aisles disappear into the distance for hundreds of metres.

'Where do we start?' you ask the Doctor.

'Trust me,' he assures you and walks confidently off down aisle 57, 'I'm a Time Lord. I have an inbuilt sense for my TARDIS.'

Ten minutes later you are back at the beginning having tried aisle 57, aisle 56, aisle 58 and aisle 42 (that had been your idea, taking a number picked at random!) without any success.

Near the door you see a small screen and keyboard and wander over to take a closer look. The screen has a simple interface and invites you to enter your search criteria. You type in a description of the TARDIS and it comes up with a location — aisle 118, section D.

Without telling the Doctor about this you suggest trying another 'random' aisle and march off to number 118.

There, in the fourth bay, you finally find the TARDIS. The Doctor is delighted and runs to open the door.

It is a great relief to get back inside the cavernous interior of the space/time machine. The constant hum of the TARDIS engines is immensely comforting.

The Doctor dashes up to the control consoles and begins making settings.

'Where to now?' you wonder.

The Doctor glances over at you. 'Home, I think — don't you?' He sees your face fall. 'But maybe we can take in the odd sight on the way, eh?'

For now, your adventure is over

20 The Doctor slides down the tube ahead of you and quickly disappears around a bend. His voice echoes back up to you.

'Come on down,' he shouts, 'it's perfectly safe!'

You jump after him and slide quickly down the tube. It's a bit like a swimming pool slide or a helter-skelter, and after all the excitement of searching for the TARDIS, it's quite fun. Your enjoyment comes to a sudden end, however, when you hurl around the final bend in the tube and find yourself flying towards the outer door of an airlock. Luckily the Doctor is waiting for you and manages to open the door before you hit it.

Inside the airlock the Doctor helps you to your feet and firmly closes the outer door.

If the airlock begins to fill with gas, go to 64. If the outer door of the airlock begins to open again, go to 5.

21 | A pair of large robots mounted on caterpillar tracks rather than legs are placing some kind of metal harness around the TARDIS. The harness crackles with energy and then, without any further warning, the harness — and the TARDIS inside it — fades from view.

'Doctor!' you cry, but he is already ahead of you, running full pelt and sliding to a stop between the robots, exactly where the TARDIS was recently standing.

'Where have you taken her?' he demands, flicking his head from side to side, trying to work out which of them is in charge. Neither robot appears to be capable of answering, or perhaps they are just not programmed to be helpful.

'What are we going to do now?' you ask the Doctor.

'We have to find someone in authority,' he tells you.

If you met a cleaner when you landed, go to 46. If you met an alien, go to 92.

'We've been told by Spaceship Traffic Control that we've lost our launch window,' announces the pilot over the intercom, 'and we'll have to stay on the launch pad for a few more minutes, but I'm certain we can make up the time when we do get underway.'

The Doctor tells you not to worry. 'We'll catch up with the TARDIS soon enough.'

'How can it already be on Saturn?' you ask. 'Surely it's only been a couple of hours since it went missing?'

'It will have gone on a Freight Express — a ship without any inertia dampeners. Unless you want to arrive looking like jam we have to take the scenic route,' explains the Doctor.

Eventually you get underway, but minutes into your flight you're shaken by a huge wave of turbulence.

If there is a sudden loss of power, go to 12. If an alarm sounds, go to 67.

'We've been hit by some kind of space mine,' the Doctor tells you.

'A weapon?' you ask.

'More of a trap,' explains the Doctor. 'It's attacking the ship's systems, unlocking the defence shields, making it easy for someone to board.'

'Someone's trying to board us?' you ask.

'Someone already has,' the Doctor tells you, as a gang of space pirates spill on to the bridge.

'If no one does anything silly, no one will get hurt,' announces the leader of the band. He introduces himself as Hawkeye Pete.

The pirates are a rough and ready bunch of wild-looking men and aliens, dressed in colourful but ragged clothes. Some have modern weapons while others are more traditional — cutlasses, swords and ancient muskets.

Hawkeye Pete announces that he is seeking something called 'the StarFire.'

If Hawkeye Pete orders you to be taken aboard the pirate ship for questioning, go to 72. If the Doctor asks a question, go to 98.

Dave (the 'cleaner' who you ran into at the Hub when you first landed) is standing in front of the TARDIS pointing a laser pistol at you.

'Oh Dave, Dave, Dave,' says the Doctor, 'what have you got yourself into?'

'You don't need to know,' says Dave tersely.

'You don't want to do this, do you?' says the Doctor. 'Why don't you just put the weapon down and we can talk about this?'

'I can't...' stutters the increasingly nervous-looking man, 'I need the money. They said they'd pay me a thousand credits. My mother's ill. She's going to die... but there's a new treatment. It's experimental,' he explains.

'And expensive?' guesses the Doctor. Dave nods.

'So who are your buyers?'

Dave looks uncertain. 'They call themselves the Collectors,' he tells you eventually.

The Doctor snorts with derision. 'You've heard of them?' Dave asks.

'Oh yes,' says the Doctor, 'the most uptight, boring bunch of nutters I've ever met. They collect everything: books, paintings, music, all sorts of things. And what do they do with it all? They encase them in plastic, write the details on a record card and file them away, never to be seen again. Collectors! I hate them.'

The Doctor comes to a halt, still fuming. 'One of these days I'm going to have to track them down and stop them for good, but right now I just want to stop them collecting my TARDIS.'

'But Dave's mum,' you remind him.

'Oh, money's no problem,' the Doctor waves an arm airily, 'I've got savings accounts in a dozen different time zones, got to love that compound interest...'

After locating some gold for Dave, and giving him a lift home, the Doctor turns to you.

'I think that's quite enough space travel for one day. Time to get you home.'

Your adventure in time and space is over.

A dozen or so armed men pour out of the lift and surround both you and the Doctor.

'At last — I was getting tired of dealing with stupid robots!' declares the leader, a rough-looking type dressed like an old-school pirate.

'That explains the skull and crossbones on that ship back there,' mutters the Doctor.

'Space pirates!' you exclaim, a little louder than you intend to.

'Why do people always call us that?' complains the man.

'Maybe it's down to the way you dress?' suggests the Doctor.

'We're just businessmen,' exclaims the man, who tells you his name is Hawkeye Pete.

'So what's with the pirate look then?' you ask, curiosity getting the better of you.

'Our accountant told us to do it. Apparently there are tax benefits,' Hawkeye Pete explains.

If Hawkeye Pete has a proposition for you, go to 96. If he threatens you, go to 62.

The smoke is getting thicker now and you struggle to breathe. You look around you, desperately searching for anything that might be an extinguisher. The medic grabs your hand.

'Help me get him out of here,' she asks you, indicating the unconscious form of the injured man.

'But the Doctor...' You are cut off before you can complete your sentence.

'He'll die unless you help me move him!'

Reluctantly you help the medic carry the injured crew member out into the corridor.

'Thank you,' the medic tells you, 'I can handle it from here.'

The doors you just came through shut automatically behind you, leaving the Doctor to cope with the smoke. You look for the control to make them open again and see a red cylinder set into an alcove.

If you get the doors to open, go to 49.
If the doors open from within, go to 4.

27 | Everything happens really quickly. The Doctor produces a credit chip which gets you two economy class tickets on the next scheduled flight and within minutes you are being ushered on-board the Star Cruiser Kestrel. The whole process is just like boarding a plane back on Earth but on a much larger scale. The docking tunnel that carries you from the waiting area to the airlock of the space craft is over three kilometres long but you are carried along it in a matter of seconds on a moving platform.

'Inertia-dampeners keep it safe,' says the Doctor, spotting the nervous look on your face.

Soon you are settled in the cramped economy class cabin. Your seat is surprisingly comfortable but the Doctor is fidgeting in his.

'I prefer to drive myself,' he tells you.

**If you launch without incident, go to 47.
If the pilot makes an announcement first, go to 22.**

28 You realise that you've been addressed by a robot. It's humanoid in shape, with a sculptured plastic face. The robot's fixed expression is strangely unsettling.

'Can we help you?' asks the Doctor, stepping forward quickly. 'I'm the Doctor and this is...' he trails off realising that you've yet to tell him your name. You introduce yourself quickly.

'I am afraid that you are in a restricted area,' the robot tells you, sternly.

'Are we?' I'm so sorry,' begins the Doctor but the robot continues.

'This is a high security access corridor — organics are strictly forbidden.'

'Organics?' you repeat, not understanding the term.

'Anything that's not strictly robotic,' explains the Doctor, 'which puts us in a bit of a pickle.'

You look back towards the place where the TARDIS landed and get a shock.

If the TARDIS has disappeared, go to 84.
If the TARDIS is being removed, go to 68.

The sensation of travel by matter transmitter is one of the strangest feelings that you've ever had. On one level it doesn't feel like you've moved at all, yet at the same time your stomach seems to flip as if you have just been upside down on a roller coaster.

You blink and when you open your eyes the room in front of you has changed subtly. The junior officer operating the controls is no longer there and the shielded console is in a different position. You step off the platform and notice that your legs are quite wobbly. A wave of nausea washes over you but you take a deep breath and soon begin to feel a bit better.

You wait but the Doctor doesn't arrive.

Without warning the door to the room opens.

If you go out to explore, go to 10. If you decide to wait, go to 100.

30 The Commander explains his plan of action to you. His team of investigators believe that the TARDIS has been sprayed with a coating of data-rich plastic. 'It sounds fantastic,' he tells you, 'but that data is crucial financial information that could be worth trillions of credits if it can be harvested.'

'So, follow the TARDIS — and it should lead you to the masterminds behind this scheme?' suggests the Doctor.

'Exactly,' the Commander agrees.

'So, how are you going to catch these people?' you ask. The Commander looks at you and smiles.

'That's where you come in as the owners of the missing box. We're travelling at maximum speed right now to get ahead of the freighter. In a little over thirty minutes we'll be arriving at StarBase Gamma and then we can lay our trap.'

If you are chosen to go undercover, go to 15. If you are asked to observe, go to 65.

You grab the white cylinder and to your surprise the medic reaches out for it.

'Thank you, he needs oxygen.' She takes the cylinder from you and pulls a face mask from a hidden panel. 'Can you help me move him?' the medic asks you, nodding at her patient, who is now breathing from the cylinder.

'But we need a fire extinguisher...' you tell her.

'Help me and I'll show you where they are.'

You nod and help the medical officer carry the man out into the corridor. The engine room doors slam shut behind you.

The medic thanks you for your help and points to the fire extinguisher. You grab the extinguisher and try to get back into the engine room.

If you find the doors to the engine room are stuck, go to 49. If the engine room doors open from within before you reach them, go to 4.

32 You step out of the TARDIS and stop in astonishment. You find yourself inside a long glass tube-like bridge suspended over a massive chamber. Below you can see long lines of desks disappearing into the distance and long queues of people standing in line, with what looks like luggage beside them. It's a noisy and busy scene. Screens flash with strange alien writing. Beyond the long lines of desks you can see shops and food stalls.

Taking all this in, you don't notice that the Doctor has stepped out behind you and locked the door of the TARDIS.

'This is the Hub,' the Doctor explains, 'the largest and busiest spaceport in the sector. Makes Heathrow look tiny, doesn't it?'

'Excuse me?' a new voice suddenly speaks behind you.

If you turn and find a man in a smart uniform, go to 45. If the speaker is a robot, go to 28.

You come round and find a blonde-haired woman leaning over you. She's holding an oxygen mask over your mouth and nose but, seeing your eyes flicker open, she pulls the mask free.

'How are you feeling?' she asks you, as you sit up.

'Where am I?' you ask. 'And where's the Doctor?'

'Which one?' asks a familiar voice. The Doctor is sitting on a couch opposite you. 'This is Doctor Sophia Virk,' he tells you, indicating the blonde woman.

Doctor Virk tells you that you are on the Space Police Cruiser Gene Hunt. You thank her for coming to your rescue.

'The police didn't come to rescue us,' explains the Doctor, 'they came to arrest us!'

The Doctor tells you that the police are investigating a smuggling ring. The police think that the gang is using the TARDIS to carry something illegally aboard the space freighter *Hulke*.

'But you've got the only key, haven't you?' you ask, confused.

The Doctor points out that the gang don't have to get inside the TARDIS to use it. 'All they have to do is fix something to it,' he says.

'So are we going to get locked up?' you wonder. The Doctor shakes his head. 'After a little chat the police believe that we're innocent victims in this affair.'

Doctor Virk tells you that you are clear to get up now. She suggests that you and the Doctor should report to the bridge, where Commander Jacoby is waiting to talk to you.

The Doctor leads the way through the ship's gleaming corridors. A pair of automatic doors slide open and you walk out on to the bridge.

If the ship comes under attack, go to 14.
If the Commander comes over to you, go to 39.

Carefully, you step out of the Pod door and into another airlock. The Doctor follows you out.

'Excellent,' he announces.

Suddenly the lights dim and a high-pitched electronic tone sounds. You cover your ears with your hands. The sound dies away and immediately you are bathed in a burst of what looks and feels like steam. After a few moments the steam vanishes but you don't appear to be damp at all.

'What was that all about?' you demand.

'That was a total decontamination scan,' the Doctor explains. 'Someone round here's pretty paranoid about bugs.'

The Doctor takes a couple of steps towards the doors leading to the rest of the ship.

'Open sesame!' commands the Doctor, giving you a wink.

To your astonishment the doors begin to open.

If someone is waiting for you, go to 99.
If the corridor beyond the door is empty,
go to 89.

You let off the fire extinguisher and, to your relief, the flames die down immediately. The Doctor is able to continue recalibrating the engines and soon announces that the crisis is over.

As things get back to normal you and the Doctor are thanked by the Captain. He promises to get you to Saturn as quickly as possible. In the meantime he instructs the crew to upgrade your accommodation and you continue the flight in the lap of luxury, in a first class cabin.

After a lovely meal and a pleasant sleep you are woken by the Doctor. It is time to disembark — you've arrived at your destination.

The Captain makes a point of seeing you off himself, wishing you well and thanking you again for saving his ship.

You step through the ship's airlock and out into a quiet arrivals area. The Doctor tells you that you are on a massive Space Station in orbit around Saturn. This is the headquarters of the Galactic SpacePort Authority who own and operate the Hub and it is here that the TARDIS should have been taken.

'All we have to do now,' the Doctor continues, 'is find her.'

You look around the arrivals hall; it's not much bigger than your school hall.

'How hard is that going to be?' you wonder.

The Doctor explains that this is the passenger arrivals area but the Space Station doesn't receive many passengers. The main part of the station is operated by robots and Artificial Intelligence units and is considerably larger.

'How much larger?' you wonder. The Doctor's reply makes you wish you hadn't asked.

If the Doctor tells you that there are ten thousand kilometres of corridor here, go to 8. If he tells you that the station is the size of London, go to 95.

Suddenly a taser pistol fires and the Commander collapses on to the floor. A uniformed police officer steps out and checks that Jacoby is okay.

'Just stunned, ma'am,' he reports looking up at Doctor Virk.

'You're in charge?' you ask.

'This is Special Operations Officer Virk,' the Doctor tells you. 'She took me into her confidence when she first found us.'

'I've been undercover on this case for months,' she tells you, 'but now, thanks to your help, we can label this one closed.'

You remind the Doctor that you have some unfinished business.

'We still don't know where the TARDIS is!' You point out.

Vick grins. 'The Commander had your ship placed somewhere safe in order to retrieve the smuggled data at his leisure,' she tells you.

'So where is "somewhere safe"?'

If the TARDIS is in a rubbish skip, go to 48.
If the TARDIS is in a storeroom, go to 19.

37 The ship you think is carrying the TARDIS has just docked at the Space Service Station. The Doctor explains to you that all the refuelling is done by automatic systems but there is a manual airlock system which he thinks he can use to get you on-board.

He takes his sonic screwdriver and begins to manipulate the computer systems.

An alarm begins to sound.

'Oh dear — I wasn't expecting that,' he exclaims. 'Security protocols,' he adds, 'I think I might have upset the computer,' the Doctor tells you. Ignoring the noise he makes another couple of adjustments and the airlock door opens.

Beyond it a long flexible tube leads off into space.

'With luck the ship's airlock is at the other end,' the Doctor informs you.

If you lead the way down the tube, go to 16.
If the Doctor leads the way, go to 20.

You bang on the lift doors but they refuse to open. Realising that the lift just isn't working you look around for an alternative way to get to Level Two. You spot a door leading to an emergency staircase and, moments later, you're dashing down plain concrete steps two at a time. Soon you reach Level Two and the black smoke from the explosion leads you directly to the Security Chief's office.

'Doctor?' you call, desperately. 'Doctor!'

'Over here,' comes a familiar voice and, to your great relief you see the Doctor, apparently unharmed, picking through the rubble left by the explosion. His clothes and face are smeared with grime but apart from that he seems totally unscathed.

'What happened?' you ask. 'Some kind of booby trap?'

The Doctor shrugs. 'I'm not sure. It was certainly primed to go off when we hit some kind of trip wire but there's something very odd about this.'

You can't see what the problem is and glance at Commander Jacoby, who is also there, to see if he has anything to add, but the police officer looks as confused as you are.

'What do you mean — odd?' asks Jacoby.

'Someone tried to kill you, Doctor,' you point out, when he fails to answer.

'That's just it,' replies the Doctor, suddenly animated, 'you've hit the nail on the head. Someone set a booby trap alright but it was a very benign one. There wasn't enough explosive here to kill. This was precision-made to cause property damage and not harm anyone.'

'But why would someone make a bomb like that?'

The Doctor shakes his head. 'Commander, do you have any ideas?'

If the Commander has disappeared, go to 94. If the Commander pulls a gun on you, go to 76.

39 When you step on to the bridge of the Police spaceship, a handsome man in his thirties with jet black eyes and a warm smile hurries across to you.

'All recovered from your ordeal?' Commander Jacoby enquires. His concern for your well-being encourages you to trust him. The Doctor certainly seems to have plenty of time for the young policeman.

'Jacoby... Jacoby, not related to Sean Jacoby, the Lion of the Rim Wars are you?' asks the Doctor.

'My Great Uncle!' exclaims the Commander. 'You know of him?'

'Better than that, I was there with him that day he organised the rescue of the Terran Mission on Garvan Five,' confesses the Doctor. You can see that Jacoby is impressed, but puzzled.

'But that was fifty years ago,' he says.

'I moisturise,' the Doctor informs him.

If the ship is attacked, go to 14. If the Commander explains his plan, go to 30.

40 'It's no good,' the Doctor tells you, 'I can't get a ticket for the Express. So we'll just have to ride without one.'

'Okay, but if we get caught, it was your idea!' you tell him.

'We have to get the TARDIS back,' he reminds you.

He then uses his psychic paper to get you both on-board the Express.

'It tells people what they expect to see,' he explains, 'in this case, that you and I are Safety Inspectors.'

The Express ship is dark, dirty and very crowded and it's quite a relief when the ship makes its first stop and the Doctor leads the way out. While you get used to the zero gravity the Doctor checks on your surroundings and makes a nasty discovery.

If he tells you that you are on a Space Beacon, go to 3. If he tells you that you are on an Automated Fuel Store, go to 58.

The Doctor sets off at a healthy pace and you are forced to jog to keep up with him.

'Nothing like a brisk walk every day to keep you fit,' he tells you with a contented grin.

'But this is nothing like a brisk walk,' you point out, 'it's more like a slow run!'

The Doctor laughs, apologises and slows down. 'When we reach the main part of the station there'll be some rapid transport system — vacuum lifts probably, if I remember this design rightly. You can't expect anyone to walk that far!' You're relieved to hear it and even happier when the Doctor tells you he can see a station.

You've reached a more populous area of the Space Base now and are surrounded by humans, aliens and robots of all shapes and sizes. You feel as if you're in a busy city rather than on a massive Space Station.

The vacuum-powered transit is both efficient and fast; within a few minutes you are disembarking at the dockside area for the freighter.

A customs robot is on duty at a desk near the conveyer belts, on which huge containers are being carried out of the ship's hold and into storage areas. The Doctor approaches the robot and explains why you are there.

The robot is not programmed for customer service and is quite abrupt in answering the Doctor's query. 'Negative. Subject "lost property" unknown,' it warbles in a barely comprehensible electronic voice.

'We lost a blue box at the Hub. It's meant to be on this ship,' you explain, managing to stop yourself calling it a stupid robot.

If the robot tells you there was no lost luggage on-board, go to 18. If the robot tells you the lost luggage has been moved to another ship, go to 71.

42 The Express flight back to the Hub is the least comfortable journey yet. Like a budget airline, the flight is crowded and the seats cramped. The only good thing is that it's fast. For five hours you suffer, squeezed into a tiny seat, with no entertainment and little in the way of refreshment but soon you are back where it all started — on the Hub, the biggest and most exciting spaceport in the sector, as the Doctor reminds you.

'Why am I so tired?' you complain. 'All this travel is hard work!'

The Doctor decides that you should begin by talking to the Hub authorities, but as you cross one of the busy arrivals areas you see a familiar figure.

If you met a robot when you first arrived at the Hub, go to 91. If you met a man when you first arrived at the Hub, go to 93.

43 The Doctor dashes into the TARDIS and tries to slam the door behind him, but the pirate leader is too quick for the Time Lord. He thrusts a foot into the gap and pushes hard with all his weight. Moments later Hawkeye Pete bursts into the TARDIS, sending the Doctor flying.

'Now what in the Seven Systems is this place?' he demands.

No one answers him.

'Just give yourself up, man,' the customs official suggests finally, 'you've lost.'

'What do you mean?' demands Hawkeye Pete.

'Before you captured me, I introduced a targeted computer virus into your ship's navigational systems. Your ship won't be going anywhere.'

'Then I'll take this one,' grins the pirate leader, 'but I won't be needing you.' He points his weapon at the customs officer.

If the customs official with you is human, go to 101. If the customs official is a blue-skinned alien, go to 102.

44 The blue-skinned alien, Professor Steele, is pointing a laser weapon at you. Behind him you can see the TARDIS.

'I was wondering when we'd see you again,' the Doctor says calmly.

The alien frowns. 'You were expecting me?'

'You gave yourself away,' explains the Doctor, 'when you wished us good luck in finding my TARDIS. We never used the name. So how did you know what it was?'

The Professor shrugs. 'I've done my research,' he tells you. 'I'm an academic, a historian,' he continues, 'I make sense of fragments of information, I discover the past. And dotted throughout human history are references to you, Doctor, and your magical space/time machine – the TARDIS.'

'I do try and slip away unnoticed,' the Doctor comments sadly.

'Oh, you've tried to cover your tracks, hiding behind pseudonyms, wiping records, avoiding publicity. The Bad Wolf virus was particularly effective at the start of the twenty-first century but nevertheless enough survived. Enough to make me recognise what it was when your TARDIS landed at the Hub and I knew I had to have it. Unfortunately I didn't get the key, would you mind obliging?'

To your surprise the Doctor hands over the TARDIS key and the Professor immediately tries to open the door. But as soon as the key touches the lock a blot of blue electricity dances through his body and he collapses to the floor unconscious.

The Doctor steps over him and ushers you into the console room. 'He's just stunned, don't worry. Not as clever as he thought was he? As if the old girl would let just anyone in!'

The Doctor hurries to the controls. 'I think that's enough space travel for one day, don't you? Time to get you home.'

Your adventure in time and space is over.

'Can I help you?' The man addressing you is wearing a smart blue uniform with gold highlights. Over his shoulder he has a large black leather case and under his arm he is carrying a cap.

'Captain Bertie Lacey,' he introduces himself, proffering a hand to shake. You shake and introduce yourself and the Doctor. The Captain has a neat moustache and an old-fashioned English accent.

'We're just passing through,' the Doctor tells him.

'Isn't everyone here?' Lacey replies with a grin. 'Half a million passengers every seventy-two hours,' he tells you. 'Stay here long enough and you'll see most of the known universe pass you by.'

'Can you imagine the lost luggage in here?' comments the Doctor with a smile.

You look over the Captain's shoulder and gasp in surprise.

If the TARDIS has gone, go to 84. If the TARDIS is being taken, go to 68.

46 Dave, the cleaner you met a moment ago, comes up silently behind you.

'Was that your blue box?' he asks you.

'Yes,' the Doctor tells him, 'and it's vital that we get it back as soon as possible.'

Dave pulls a face and takes a long slow intake of breath. 'You should have thought about that before you left it in a secure area.'

'Don't start that again,' you say.

'I thought you said Security would be on their way?' asks the Doctor. 'Where are they?'

The cleaner shrugs. 'Looks like they've dealt with this one remotely. You'll have to go to the Security Office now.'

'And where do we find that, then?'

'It's on Saturn, isn't it? No room on site here for it.'

If the Doctor gets you tickets on to a commercial flight to Saturn, go to 27. If the Doctor cadges a lift from another traveller, go to 82.

47 To your surprise the launch of the spaceship is almost an anticlimax — you hardly feel a thing. 'It's not like space travel in your time,' he tells you, 'with rockets reaching escape velocity in seconds and having to fight to escape the pull of the Earth's gravity.'

'It's almost as if we're not moving at all,' you comment.

The Doctor activates a screen built into the cabin wall and a display shows the Hub — which you can now see to be a giant Space Station in orbit between Earth and the Moon — receding into the distance.

'We'll get even faster in a minute when we go into hyperspeed,' he tells you.

'How will I know?' you ask him.

'They'll be a slight tremor,' says the Doctor, seconds before a massive shockwave hits, sending you flying from your seat.

If there is a sudden loss of power, go to 12. If an alarm sounds, go to 67.

'A scrap heap!' The Doctor is clearly offended and with good reason — the refuse room is a very offensive place. The officials in charge have issued you with protective clothing and a face mask but it's not enough to keep the smell of rotting waste out of your nostrils.

'If ever there was a perfect argument for recycling,' you comment, 'then surely this is it.'

The Doctor is moving slowly in front of you, shifting bags of rubbish aside. 'You may have a point,' he agrees.

The refuse room is an area the size of a football field, covered with litter bags, loose rubbish and larger items like old communicator screens and personal fridges. It's like the local dump back home but without any attempt to recycle.

'Ah, there she is,' he announces, pointing into the distance, where you can just make out the blue of the TARDIS police box exterior sticking out from behind a pile of black bin bags.

The Doctor clears a path for you both and, after a good deal of effort you reach the time/space machine and the Doctor manages to get the door open.

It is a relief to get inside the TARDIS where you can get out of the protective overalls and uncomfortable boots.

The Doctor hops over to the console and starts up the engines.

'I'm going to need a car wash,' he jokes, as he programmes the destination coordinates into the flight computers.

'Where are we going then?' you ask hopefully.

The Doctor sits back in his chair and gives you a long look.

'I think you've done quite enough travelling for the time being, don't you?'

You can't help feeling a bit disappointed.

'Do I have to go home?' you wonder.

The Doctor grins. 'Let's see where we end up, shall we?'

Your adventure is over — for now.

49 You are overcome with black, dense smoke as soon as the doors begin to open. Coughing, you fall to the floor.

'Doctor?' you call out, but there is no answer from within.

Looking into the room from your prone position you realise that the smoke is not quite as thick at floor level. You can see a body lying close to the doors and for a moment fear that it must be the Doctor. You and the medic dash inside the door and pull the unconscious junior engineer out into the corridor.

With the doors open the smoke in the room begins to dissipate a little and you can make out a shape still standing at the control console — it looks like the Doctor is trying to fix the problem.

If you get the fire extinguisher to the Doctor, go to 13. If you start using the fire extinguisher, go to 35.

The automatic launch process starts up the moment the door locks closed.

'Emergency Escape Pod Activated,' says a calm female voice, 'please ensure that you have engaged all safety straps. Launch in twenty seconds. Standard launch trajectory will be observed.'

'Don't worry,' the Doctor tells you. 'I've made a few adjustments...'

Suddenly the capsule begins to rumble and shake and then, with an explosion, it is launched. The capsule spins crazily and you feel a tremendous force pinning you to the couch. And then, as quickly as it began, the spinning slows to a gentle rock and the pressure falls away.

'So far so good,' comments the Doctor.

Suddenly you hear something metallic crunching outside the capsule.

'We've been picked up,' the Doctor tells you and moments later the capsule door begins to open.

If the Doctor leads the way, go to 17.
If you go first, go to 34.

A new voice continues the story.

'Then the contraband is sent with the lost luggage out here to StarBase Gamma, where it finds its way to the Commander and his clients.'

You turn and see that it is the Doctor who saved your life earlier — Doctor Virk. She is also now holding a laser pistol in her hand, but hers is pointing directly at Jacoby.

'Virk, I didn't realise you knew about all this,' Jacoby begins, a note of desperation in his voice, 'but I can cut you in on it, just don't let the Doctor stick a spanner in the works.'

'Sorry,' says the medic, 'no deal.'

The Doctor is looking behind the Commander. 'Keep back,' he calls out.

Jacoby laughs. 'You think I'm going to fall for that old trick?'

If you shout out a warning, go to 78. If he is shot from behind, go to 36.

You see that the man who addressed you is an unassuming middle-aged man wearing dark blue overalls, holding a bucket and a mop. The laminated ID card hanging round his neck reveals that his name is Dave.

'Er, sorry to interrupt you, but you really aren't meant to be here,' he says, slightly nervously.

'No need to apologise,' the Doctor assures the cleaner, 'just point us in the right direction.'

'But this is a secure area,' Dave insists. 'Security will already be on their way.'

'Security? I don't like the sound of that,' you comment.

'Don't worry. I'm always getting arrested for this kind of misunderstanding,' the Doctor tells you, trying to reassure you.

Looking over the Doctor's shoulder you see something quite disturbing.

If the TARDIS has disappeared, go to 87.
If you see a metallic grasp picking up the TARDIS, go to 21.

53 The cell is a tiny room with metal walls and no window. There is no furniture other than a slab of metal on concrete blocks, forming a primitive bench. The Doctor sits, puts his feet up and leans back.

'As prison cells go, I've seen worse,' he announces, apparently not at all worried about being locked up.

'You get imprisoned a lot, do you?' you ask him, surprised at how casually he is taking this development.

He scratches an itch behind his ear and screws his face up. 'S'pose I do really. Don't know why. But I don't usually stay for long.'

Before you can ask what he means the door opens and a figure you recognise appears.

**If this is the blue-skinned alien, Professor Steele, who you met on the Hub, go to 66.
If it is the cleaner 'Dave' who you met on the Hub, go to 6.**

54 The lift seems to take forever to plummet to the bottom of the lift shaft.

'What's at the bottom of the Space Station?' you ask.

'The arrivals area for the larger ships,' the Doctor tells you. The doors opens and he leads you out into a central area from which six opaque corridors stretch out into space. There are gantries at regular intervals along each arm, some of which are occupied with various kinds of spaceship.

The Doctor begins to lead you out along one of the arms. The further out from the station you go, the better the view is. Looking back you can see the huge bulk of the station rising up like a massive skyscraper from the central hub where you came from.

If the Doctor sees something move on one of the ships, go to 56. If you see some movement back at the lifts, go to 25.

55 The Doctor steps on to the platform and gives you an encouraging wink.

'It's a bit unpleasant but don't worry — it won't kill you.' The officer operates the controls and the Doctor fades from view. A split-second later he becomes solid again, adds, 'Well, not often,' and then disappears again, this time permanently.

Now it is your turn. You close your eyes and cross your fingers. For a moment nothing seems to happen but then you get a strange feeling washing over your body and a peculiar lightness, as if for a tiny moment you don't have a physical body at all.

You open your eyes and find that you have been transported to a similar but different room. The Doctor, however, is not here waiting for you.

The door to the room is open.

If you go out to explore, go to 10. If you decide to wait, go to 100.

56 Some figures are moving at the entrance to one of the gantries. The ship moored there is painted black and battle-scarred. For some reason you have a bad feeling about the ship and its crew. And then you realise why. There is a familiar-looking flag painted on the bow of the ship — a skull and crossbones.

'Space pirates!' you exclaim as, suddenly, a dozen or so humans spill out from the ship and surround you.

'Actually we prefer "freelance entrepreneurs" these days,' says the group's leader, a swarthy-looking man dressed in a stripy top and wearing an eye patch.

'So the fancy costumes and the skull and crossbones?' asks the Doctor.

'Just something we do for fun,' says the man who goes on to introduce himself as Hawkeye Pete.

**If Hawkeye Pete has a proposition for you,
go to 96. If he threatens you, go to 62.**

57 | The cell that you are thrown into is completely dark. There are no windows and, once the door is locked behind you, there is no immediate source of light.

'Don't panic,' the Doctor whispers to you, 'they took my sonic screwdriver but...' he pauses and there is a rustle of fabric and some grunting followed by a click and a small beam of light, 'ah, there we are, I knew I had a torch in one of these pockets.'

He waves the torch beam around the room, which is quite large and sparsely furnished. At the rear of the room is a bed on which is a figure waking from sleep. It's someone you know.

If this is the blue-skinned alien, Professor Steele, who you met on the Hub, go to 66. If it is the cleaner 'Dave' who you met on the Hub, go to 6.

'Is this really StarBase Gamma?' you ask, looking around at the cramped Space Station.

The Doctor shakes his head, a serious expression on his face.

'No, we've made a terrible mistake,' he tells you. 'This is just an automated fuel dump.'

'Like a Space Service Station?' you suggest.

The Doctor shrugs. 'Sort of. But there's no shop, no fast food outlets. In fact not a lot in the way of life support.'

'But there's oxygen — we're breathing.'

'For now,' the Doctor tells you, 'but this station isn't designed for human occupation. The oxygen supply is limited.'

Before long you begin to notice that the air is getting thin. Are you going to die here, in the middle of nowhere, in the distant future? Everything begins to turn black.

If you come round inside a spaceship, go to 33. If you come round still in the same place, go to 70.

The Doctor continues the story.

'The data, or whatever it is to be smuggled, gets added to the lost luggage and it's all sent here to StarBase Gamma where the specially programmed stevedore robots retrieve the contraband and collect for the Commander and his clients.' The Doctor pauses and looks at Jacoby. 'Is that about the size of it?'

'Very good, Doctor,' the Commander compliments your companion, 'but now I'm afraid that I'm going to have to kill you. Simply put, you know too much,' he tells you.

'I wouldn't do that, if I were you,' states a new voice. The medical officer, Doctor Virk appears, also carrying a weapon in her hand.

Jacoby is deeply unimpressed. 'Oh please, what is this? A mutiny?'

You see a movement behind him.

If you shout out a warning, go to 78. If he is shot from behind, go to 36.

The lift doors open and you step out into a very different-looking area of the Space Station. You are at the end of a long corridor, the curved ceiling of which is completely transparent. You can see deep space and the bright coloured shape of the nearby Saturn and, further along the corridor, a number of docking ports.

'Interesting,' comments the Doctor, checking the reading from his TARDIS detector. 'Maybe the old girl is still on one of these ships rather than somewhere on the station.'

And now, as you look more carefully at the various gantries, you can see that a number of them are occupied with various spacecraft.

'Let's take a closer look,' suggests the Doctor and leads you further away from the lift area.

If you see some movement from one of the ships, go to 56. If someone appears behind you, go to 25.

The Doctor looks at the screen in horror. 'They're not stopping!' he exclaims. 'It's no good, we'll have to do this the hard way, follow me.' He gets up and runs out of the room. You hurry after him.

'A station like this will have emergency escape pods,' he yells back over his shoulder as you tear through the station, 'the guidance systems will be primitive but good enough to launch us into the slipstream of that ship. They'll have to pick us up.'

He reaches a door surrounded by red labels saying 'DANGER' and 'EMERGENCY USE ONLY'. He opens the door and gestures you inside.

You find a cramped capsule with three moulded padded couches. 'Strap yourself in,' orders the Doctor.

The Doctor slams the double doors shut.

If the capsule launches automatically, go to 50. If the capsule fails to activate, go to 74.

Hawkeye Pete's expression hardens and he takes a step closer. 'You need to understand that we have been wandering around this dump for a long time and had no one to talk to except a lot of very stupid robots, which we've had great pleasure in blasting into atoms. But we're running out of patience now so I'm going to make this nice and simple for you.'

He leans in and looks you directly in the eyes.

'The StarFire. Do you know where it is?'

You shake your head. 'What about you?' roars the man, turning to the Doctor.

'I don't even know what it is,' the Doctor tells him honestly.

Hawkeye's eyes narrow with anger. He has his men take you on to his ship where you are thrown into a cell.

If the cell is empty, go to 53. If the cell is already occupied, go to 57.

The robot you met earlier steps forward.

'I am authorised to assist organics if they become lost or confused,' he tells you. He offers to locate the TARDIS and then suddenly freezes.

'What's it doing?' you ask, in a whisper.

'Communicating with the Hub's computers, wireless technology of course,' explains the Doctor also in a whisper, adding, 'why are we whispering?'

Suddenly the robot's head snaps straight again.

'I have located your box,' he tells you, 'it has been removed from the Hub on the space freighter *Hulke* en route for StarBase Gamma.'

'Can we get on that ship?' asks the Doctor.

The robot shakes his head. 'Space freighters are automated, no organics,' he tells you, 'but you might try the Alpha Proxima Express — that has a fuel stop scheduled at StarBase Gamma.'

If you succeed in getting tickets, go to 85.
If you can't get a ticket, go to 40.

64 You hear a hissing sound and looking down you see some kind of milky white gas flowing into the airlock from a dozen vents in the floor.

Almost instantly you find yourself coughing.

'Someone really doesn't like us!' you manage to splutter. The Doctor has pulled his trusty sonic screwdriver from his pocket. 'Try and hold your breath,' he instructs you and then begins attacking the inner door controls with his sonic screwdriver. Nothing seems to work so he drops to the floor and directs the multi-purpose tool at the vents. To your surprise the vents click shut and the flow of gas is halted.

The Doctor stands up and helps you to your feet too. 'Right then — where's the door control?' he mutters, jabbing at some controls with his thumb.

If the inner door opens, go to 89. If the inner door fails to open, go to 99.

When you arrive at StarBase Gamma everything happens very quickly. A room is commandeered to serve as a temporary operations centre and a team of police technicians quickly kit it out with wireless surveillance equipment. A technician shows you how they have tapped into the regular closed circuit television cameras of the station's security service.

On some screens you can watch the arrivals area of the station, where the freighter *Hulke* has just docked. Specialist robots roll forward to begin removing the container pods from the ship.

On another screen you can see the Doctor, with a pair of police officers, approaching the security offices.

'The security chief is on his way to the docking area,' you report, whispering into the headset microphone you've been given, 'the office should be empty.'

If the Doctor's party walk directly into the office, go to 90. If the office is locked, go to 86.

It is Professor Steele, the blue-skinned academic that you met on the Hub. The alien confesses that he is really working for the Federation Customs Authority. He was undercover to shut down the pirate operation but got discovered.

The Doctor comes up with a plan to trick the pirates.

When Hawkeye Pete returns, the Doctor explains that you can give him the StarFire but first you need access to your blue box.

Under armed guard you are all taken to a hold where, to your delight, you find the TARDIS. The Doctor opens the door and sends you and Commander Steele in to 'fetch' the StarFire.

'Maybe I'd better give them a hand,' he suggests after a moment, but Hawkeye Pete makes a move towards the door himself.

If the Doctor manages to join you inside, go to 43. If the pirate leader gets into the TARDIS, go to 75.

| A strident alarm fills the air. 'What is it?' you ask the Doctor.

'Red alert, purple alert, some colour alert,' he tells you tensely, 'whatever it is, it's bad news.'

The Doctor is already on his feet and running from the cabin. You follow him and find yourselves on the flight deck. It's a compact area made up of various work stations but not many of them are occupied at present. In front of the main command chair a male figure in a smart uniform is lying slumped on the floor. A headset built into the back of his chair is smoking.

A medic dressed in a white tunic appears, carrying a compact emergency medical kit.

'Bio-feedback from that stupid headset,' she mutters, as she begins to attend to his wounds.

'Direct access to the ship's computers?' the Doctor asks, looking at the headset curiously.

The medic nods. 'Downright dangerous if you ask me, but I'm just the woman charged with looking after the crew's health and safety. Why should they listen to me?'

The Doctor is already sitting in the chair and pushing his head back into the headset. Motion detectors activate with a click and tiny probes extend from the headset and press contact points into the Doctor's skin.

'Let's see if I can get this to work,' mutters the Doctor.

Suddenly the alarm stops and the Doctor's eyes snap open. 'That's better. Now then, let's see what's going on, shall we?' He closes his eyes and consults with the computer again. Moments later his eyes open again and he jumps up from the seat.

'It shouldn't be possible but somehow the ship has been hit by something.'

If you've been hit by another spaceship, go to 97. If you've hit something in space, go to 23.

As you watch, the TARDIS is bathed in multicoloured lights that appear from nowhere.

'What's happening?' you ask the Doctor, but before he can answer it becomes quite clear — as clear as the TARDIS itself as it begins to lose its solid shape, becoming transparent and then fading completely from view.

The Doctor looks a bit stunned.

'But what are we going to do? Where has it gone?' you ask him, in a frightened tone.

'Don't panic,' the Doctor reassures you, 'I've never lost the old girl before.' He stops himself and reconsiders. 'Well, when I say never, I mean not much. Well, actually, quite a bit. But never for long. Well, when I say long...'

'Doctor, can we just find it?' you ask him, interrupting.

If you met a robot when you landed, go to 63. If you met a man when you landed, go to 83.

The speaker is a short, chubby, blue-skinned humanoid wearing a garish Hawaiian shirt that is a riot of red, yellow and orange.

'Do you folks know the way down to the Sol System Spaceways check-in desk?' asks the alien, who tells you his name is Professor Artemis Steele. You introduce the Doctor and yourself.

The Doctor explains that you've only just arrived yourselves and suggests you all look around for an information point.

'They look something like a small wall-mounted cash machine. There should be loads of them round here,' he tells you. Unfortunately most of the bridge is completely transparent — and the only wall on which you might find an information point is back in the alcove where the TARDIS landed.

When you look in that direction you have a nasty shock.

If the TARDIS has vanished, go to 87. If you see the TARDIS being taken, go to 21.

70 When you wake up you find that you are still where you were. The Doctor is kneeling over you.

'There you are! Feeling a bit better now?'

'What happened?'

'First there was no air, you passed out; then there was air and you woke up,' explains the Doctor simply. 'Nothing like a touch of oxygen, eh? Bet you never thought breathing could be such a delight!'

The Doctor gently helps you to your feet and you see that you have been joined by a couple of people in smart blue uniforms. A pleasant-looking blonde woman wearing a similar uniform and a plain white jacket is also with you.

'This is Doctor Virk,' says the Doctor, waving a hand towards the woman, 'she's with the police.'

'The police?' you repeat in a worried tone.

The Doctor tells you that a Police spaceship arrived at the Beacon just in time to bring the automatic life support systems back online.

'Thank you,' you say to the police doctor, 'lucky you turned up when you did.'

'Luck had nothing to do with it,' she replies, 'we were following you!'

You look over at the Doctor. Did you hear the woman correctly? Seeing your concern, Doctor Virk explains that the police are on the trail of a massive smuggling ring.

'But we're not smugglers,' you insist. The Doctor assures you that he has persuaded the police that you are innocent. 'The police believe the smugglers are using the TARDIS as a way to transport something illegally. We need to go on-board the Police spaceship and speak to Commander Jacoby, the officer in charge.'

If the ship comes under attack when you reach the bridge, go to 14. If the Commander comes over to you when you reach the command deck, go to 39.

You have been told that the TARDIS has been taken to a private yacht owned by the media superstar Earl.

'He's a big, big star,' the Doctor tells you, 'bigger than the Beatles, bigger than Elvis or Elvis 2,' explains the Doctor.

'Elvis 2?'

'They cloned him in the twenty-fourth century,' the Doctor tells you, 'but it wasn't quite the same. Did a great cover of Robbie Williams' *Let Me Entertain You*, though.'

The Doctor and you reach the pier at which the Earl's hyper-luxurious space yacht is moored. Dark-suited, sunglasses wearing security men stand guard, but the Doctor flashes his psychic paper at them and you're waved straight through.

'If anyone asks, we're here to do his lordship's hair,' whispers the Doctor.

If you are shown into a room where the Earl is, go to 80. If you are shown into an empty room, go to 77.

While the search for the StarFire continues you are taken aboard the pirates' spacecraft.

It is a rundown ship that shows signs of numerous running repairs, often with parts and fittings that do not match the rest of the ship. The two pirates escorting you and the Doctor couldn't be more different. One is a giant-sized human, nearly seven feet tall. He has a bald head but makes up for his lack of hair with a massive moustache that hangs down to his knees. On each earlobe he has a large dangling earring. The other pirate is an alien, with green scaly skin and four arms. The Doctor asks them politely what the StarFire is.

The human ignores the question and the alien just laughs manically.

**If you are put into an empty cell, go to 53.
If the cell you are put in is occupied, go to 57.**

The lift doors open and you jab at the floor two button with your thumb. The doors shut and you feel your stomach lurch as it jerks into action. Before you even have time to grab hold of the handrail the lift comes to an abrupt halt. You fear that there might be some kind of problem with the mechanism but then the doors open and you realise that you've arrived at your destination.

You run out of the lift and follow the trail of smoke which leads to the place where the explosion went off. To your relief, you find the Doctor examining the mess, a little sooty but undamaged.

'Doctor!' you cry out, 'I was worried about you!'

The Doctor tries to look casual, and brushes some debris off his coat. 'Oh, I've been in worse explosions,' he assures you, 'much worse than that. In fact...' he stops and glances at Commander Jacoby, who is also there.

'Yes?' he says keenly, 'have you noticed something?'

'Something doesn't add up about this,' the Doctor mutters, turning back to the rubble.

'Someone tried to kill you, don't tell me it's the first time,' you say to him.

'But that's just it,' he replies, turning to look at you with earnest eyes, 'someone didn't try to kill me. There was just enough explosive to cause this mess but not enough to harm anyone. It was just for show...'

'Why would anyone want to make it look as if someone was trying to kill you?' you wonder.

The Doctor considers for a moment, stroking his chin and unwittingly leaving a black smudge mark.

'Let's ask the Commander, shall we?' he suggests finally.

If the Commander has disappeared, go to 94. If the Commander pulls a gun on you, go to 76.

'It should launch automatically,' the Doctor tells you, but nothing happens.

'Perhaps it needs a bit of encouragement,' he suggests and fires the sonic screwdriver at the controls.

Immediately you feel the Pod beginning to shake and tremble. 'Don't panic,' the Doctor tells you, 'it's just reversing the polarity of the magnetic hull. When the restraining bolts blow, the repulsion effect will launch us into space.'

The countdown reaches zero and you are thrust back into the padded couch as the Pod shoots out of the launch tube at an incredible speed.

After a few long seconds, the pressure drops. The Doctor checks your position. 'Right next to the ship,' he tells you. Moments later you feel a slight jolt as the ship hauls you inside.

Soon the capsule door is opening.

If the Doctor leads the way, go to 17.
If you go first, go to 34.

The Doctor dives into the TARDIS but it is too late — Hawkeye Pete is already through the doors and halfway across the vast control room of the space/time craft.

'Now this is what I call treasure,' he screams, whirling around the central console, taking in the alien wonder that is the TARDIS. 'Bigger on the inside than the outside, what other magic can it do?'

'It's just a trick,' the Doctor tells him, 'an old fairground illusion. But that's all. Might be good in a travelling show but it's no bearded lady!'

The pirate leader grins, and points his weapon directly at him.

'Don't take me for a fool,' he says coldly, 'tell me all about this machine or I'll shoot you!"

The Doctor just looks at him.

If the customs official with you is human, go to 101. If the customs official is a blue-skinned alien, go to 102.

76 | To your surprise you see that the Commander has pulled a weapon out of his belt and is pointing it directly at you.

'Commander, what are you doing? We're not the criminals,' you state, feeling alarmed.

'That's not the reason he's doing it,' the Doctor tells you calmly.

'Oh, very good, very smart. I suppose you've worked it all out, have you?' the Commander asks the Doctor, in a voice dripping with sarcasm.

'Not quite all but enough,' the Doctor tells him.

'The Commander's behind the smuggling?' you ask, trying to keep up with what's going on.

'It's a perfect set-up: my friends on the Hub make sure bits and pieces of luggage get lost and then pack them alongside goods and data that aren't cleared for export...' the Commander begins.

If the Doctor completes the plot, go to 59. If a new voice picks up the story, go to 51.

You find yourselves in an ornate drawing room. If you didn't know you were on a spaceship you'd think you were in an old-fashioned French palace.

A door opens and the Earl appears. He's a handsome man in his twenties.

'Doctor!' he exclaims, before embracing him in a huge bear hug.

You jump to your feet. 'You never said you knew him,' you complain.

'Didn't I?' says the Doctor, his eyes twinkling.

The Earl wonders what's brought the Doctor to see him today. The Doctor tells him the whole story.

'Oh dear,' says the Earl. 'My people did take some lost luggage from the *Hulke* — I like to try and salvage things for charity — but this batch was all rubbish.'

'So where is it all now?' asks the Doctor.

If the TARDIS is in a rubbish skip, go to 48.
If the TARDIS is in a storeroom, go to 19.

'Look out!' you cry, but it's too late and a weapon blast fires from the darkness. A uniformed police officer steps out from the shadows and stands over the stunned Jacoby. While Virk and the police officer secure their prisoner, the Doctor explains that Virk is an undercover police operative.

'I came clean to the Doctor when I first met you,' she confesses 'but I didn't have the chance to tell you. Sorry,' she adds.

The Doctor looks pleased. 'I take it your people will round up all his associates now?'

'Happening even as we speak,' she assures him.

'Which just leaves one problem,' you remind the Doctor, 'we still haven't found the TARDIS.'

'Oh, I think I can help you with that,' says Virk.

If she tells you that the TARDIS is in a rubbish skip, go to 48. If the TARDIS is in a storeroom, go to 19.

The Doctor puts on the charm and explains that as your legal guardian he can't let you travel alone. The ruse seems to work because after further review the travel agent is able to source two tickets on the flight. The delay has been costly however, and you have to run to make the gate before the boarding closes.

Once on-board the cramped and over-crowded express flight is not pleasant, but it's also very fast and the journey only takes five hours.

'I'll never take the convenience of travel by TARDIS for granted again,' complains the Doctor, as you disembark back at the Hub. 'What a tedious way to get anywhere!'

Unexpectedly you see a figure that you recognise.

If you met a robot when you first arrived at the Hub, go to 91. If you met a man when you first arrived at the Hub, go to 93.

To your surprise the Earl is a diminutive human with a large nose and no hair.

'Hairdressers?' he asks, looking sternly at the Doctor. Your heart sinks — this is not going to plan.

'Well, it was worth a try!' says the Doctor with a laugh.

'You're losing your touch, Doctor,' says the Earl.

'You know him?' you exclaim.

'The Doc here was my first manager,' the Earl explains.

The Doctor quickly explains your situation.

'Oh yes,' says the Earl, 'I often pick up job lots of lost luggage. I run huge Bring and Buy sales to raise money for my favourite charities. But the stuff from the *Hulke* was rather poor.'

The Earl looks a little embarrassed. 'We decided to junk it.'

'So where is it now?' you ask.

If the TARDIS is in a rubbish skip, go to 48.
If the TARDIS is in a storeroom, go to 19.

'What are you looking for, kid?' the man asks you, chewing gum.

'A blue box,' you tell him, 'it was on the *Hulke*!'

The man checks a small hand-held computer and then shakes his head.

'Nothing like that on any of my lists. Sorry.'

'It was taken from the Hub, by mistake. Some idiot robot thought it was lost luggage,' you tell him.

'Lost luggage? Then you'd better talk to the Security Chief — his office is on level two.'

In your ear you can hear the Doctor. 'We're on our way there now, meet us there. Use lift shaft 10.'

A minute or two later you hear the sound of an explosion. You look around but it was in your ear not anywhere near you.

Seeing a sign for lift shaft 10 you set off at a run.

If the lift is working, go to 73. If the lift isn't working, go to 38.

To your embarrassment, the Doctor begins going up to people and asking them outright if they can offer you a lift, but despite his charm he gets little success. Then he spots a smartly-dressed woman talking on a wrist communicator.

'As soon as the pilot gets back we're cleared to take off,' the woman is saying in clipped tones, 'we'll be with you on Saturn in six hours.'

The Doctor sidles up to her and gives her his biggest grin.

'I don't mean to be nosy but I couldn't help overhearing that you're en route for Saturn,' he begins adding hopefully. 'I don't suppose you've room for two hitchhikers, have you?'

A few minutes later you're boarding a luxurious space yacht, *The Clint Eastwood*, owned by your new friend, Lady Bryon.

If you launch without incident, go to 47.
If the pilot makes an announcement first, go to 22.

83 | **C**aptain Lacey offers to help you.

'Let me get on to CENCOM,' he suggests, 'see what I can find out.' He activates a communicator and steps away from you.

'What's CENCOM?' you wonder.

'Central Computer, I would imagine,' the Doctor tells you. 'You'd need some serious computer power to keep a place like this running smoothly.'

Captain Lacey steps back towards you, smiling.

'Well the good news is that I've tracked down your box,' he tells you, 'but the bad news is that it's on a space freighter — the *Hulke* — which leaves for StarBase Gamma in twenty minutes.'

'We have to get on that ship,' states the Doctor.

'Impossible,' Lacey shakes his head, 'but if you hurry you might get seats on the next Alpha Proxima Express — that stops at the StarBase.'

If you succeed in getting tickets, go to 85.
If you can't get a ticket, go to 40.

The spot where the TARDIS was standing is now completely empty. You can't believe your eyes.

'But it was here, just a moment ago,' you mutter.

'And before that it wasn't,' comments the Doctor.

'What?' The Doctor is confusing you.

'We materialised in thin air, that's how the TARDIS lands. Now someone else has either pulled off the same trick or has a very quiet and quick crane to hand. The question is — who?'

'Shouldn't we try and locate where the TARDIS has gone before we go and find someone to blame?' you suggest calmly.

The Doctor shakes his head. 'Find the "who" and the how, which, why and where will follow,' he tells you confidently.

'So let's start getting some answers,' you suggest.

If you met a robot when you landed, go to 63. If you met a man when you landed, go to 83.

The Doctor manages to get you tickets and you find yourselves boarding the Alpha Proximi Express. It's dark and cramped and very crowded. It reminds you of a London tube train in the rush hour; a horrid crush of people.

The journey is far from comfortable and seems to take forever but, in fact, it's just a couple of hours before the Doctor leads you through the airlock into a Space Station. Immediately you feel yourself beginning to float.

'No gravity,' the Doctor tells you. Soon the Express has taken off again, leaving you and the Doctor alone.

'Why didn't anyone else get off here?' you wonder.

'Oh no,' says the Doctor in a worried tone, 'I don't think we want to be here.'

If he tells you that you are on a Space Beacon, go to 3. If he tells you that you are on an Automated Fuel Store, go to 58.

The Doctor attempts to open the door but the handle refuses to move. Watching on the surveillance camera you cannot hear anything that is being said but you recognise the Doctor's cheerful and confident grin as he reaches inside his pocket to look for his sonic screwdriver.

The Doctor makes an adjustment to his multi-purpose tool and fires a blast of concentrated sound in the direction of the lock.

Without any warning the door explodes in a flash of flames and smoke.

The screen you were watching turns to static and the nearby cameras also go down. There is no way to see if the Doctor is okay.

'How do I get down there?' you demand of the nearest police technician.

'Lift shaft 10, level two,' he tells you as you race out the door.

If you find the lift working, go to 73. If the lift isn't working, go to 38.

The TARDIS had landed in a small alcove at the back of the passageway but now that alcove is completely empty. You run into it, arms outstretched, in case there is some kind of optical illusion going on, but there is nothing there — the TARDIS has completely vanished. And without the TARDIS there is no way for you to get home!

You feel a horrible cold shiver down your spine. What if you never get home?

The Doctor pats you on the back. 'Don't worry,' he says in a reassuring tone, 'this sort of thing is always happening to me. We'll get the old girl back, never fear!'

'But where is it? And who took it. And why?' you ask.

'Good questions all,' the Doctor winks at you. 'Let's get some answers.'

If you met a cleaner when you landed, go to 46. If you met an alien, go to 92.

88 You hurry back to the room in which you arrived and are delighted and relieved to see the Doctor.

'What happened to you?' you ask.

The Doctor shrugs and runs a hand through his tangle of hair. 'I must have got held up in the transfer buffers,' he tells you.

'What's that mean?' you ask.

'Techno babble,' the Doctor explains, 'you really don't want to know. Right, is this StarBase Gamma then? Have you taken a look around?'

You explain that you just saw a freighter dock that might have been the *Hulke* and when you show the Doctor he nods. 'That's the *Hulke* alright — now all we have to do is go there and find the TARDIS.'

You look at the distant freighter and wonder how you can get there.

If the Doctor finds an electronic car, go to 7. If you set off on foot, go to 41.

The Doctor quickly leads you through the mostly empty corridors of the spaceship. 'The passengers will be in the main cabin area,' he explains, 'this is a crew and cargo area.' The only crew you encounter are basic function robots, who pay you no attention.

'Where are we going?' you ask the Doctor.

He shows you a small perspex triangle filled with slowly flashing blue lights. 'TARDIS detector,' he tells you. 'She's not far away.'

You reach a large door which is marked Cargo Bay 5. It's locked but the sonic screwdriver soon deals with that and the doors open to reveal the TARDIS.

You both start to run towards the ship but stop as a figure steps out from behind it.

If it is 'Dave' the cleaner you met on the Hub, go to 24. If it is Professor Steele who you met on the Hub, go to 44.

The Doctor and the agents move through the unlocked door and disappear from your screens.

'Isn't there a camera in the office itself?' you ask the Commander.

He frowns. 'Yes, camera twenty-four. Let me punch it up.'

He reaches across you to operate the controls which bring the image from camera twenty-four to your main screen.

'That's odd,' you comment, 'the room looks completely empty — but we just saw the Doctor going in there, didn't we?'

The Commander looks worried and reaches for his intercom.

'All units check on——' but before he can complete the sentence you hear a massive explosion from the speaker. The Commander sees your concerned expression.

'Let's get down there,' he suggests, 'we need lift shaft 10, level two will get us right there.'

If you find the lift working, go to 73. If the lift isn't working, go to 38.

'Look Doctor,' you shout grabbing his arm, 'isn't that the robot that told us where to go?'

The Doctor looks in the direction you are pointing but doesn't seem convinced.

'I don't know,' he confesses, 'these porter 'bots all look the same to me.'

'No, it's the one,' you insist, 'I remember it had a dent on the side.'

The robot itself has spotted you now, and to your delight it rolls right up to you.

'Human youth and human-type adult, I have been trying to locate you,' it announces.

'You've been looking for us?'

'I needed to correct an error. Your lost property was not loaded on to the freighter *Hulke* at all, in fact it remains on the Hub itself.'

'So where is it?' asks the Doctor.

If the TARDIS is in a rubbish skip, go to 48.
If the TARDIS is in a storeroom, go to 19.

Professor Steele has found an information point, which tells him exactly where to find his check-in desk.

'I have to run,' he tells you, 'my flight to Saturn leaves in thirty minutes. But I wish you well with your hunt. I do hope you find your TARDIS.'

He disappears at a run before you can even say goodbye.

'Oh, that's interesting,' mutters the Doctor, who is now looking at the information point.

'What is it?' you ask him.

The Doctor looks up and you see he has produced a pair of dark-rimmed glasses from somewhere.

'The TARDIS has been removed by security. We'll have to collect it from the Security Office.'

'Where's that?'

'Saturn!'

'How do we get there?' you ask.

If the Doctor gets you tickets on to a commercial flight to Saturn, go to 27. If the Doctor cadges a lift from another traveller, go to 82.

'Look!' you shout pointing, 'it's Captain Lacey.'

You hurry over to the Captain who is amazed to see you.

'I've been looking for you two,' he tells you, 'but I heard you'd gone off station.'

'Yes,' says the Doctor, with a little steeliness in his voice, 'we hurried off after the freighter *Hulke* but it turned out to be a bit of a wild goose chase.'

'Why did you send us the wrong way?'

Captain Lacey shrugs, 'I didn't. The computer did. There was an error in the lost luggage data.'

To your surprise the Doctor laughs.

'So you're saying the Hub lost the lost luggage?'

Captain Lacey nods. 'You could say that.'

'So where is the TARDIS?' you wonder.

'Ah,' says the Captain, looking even more embarrassed.

If the TARDIS is in a rubbish skip, go to 48.
If the TARDIS is in a storeroom, go to 19.

'He was right here a minute ago,' you tell the Doctor.

The Doctor gets to his feet, 'Then he can't have gone far.'

He runs off down the corridor and around a corner. You follow and crash into his back. The Doctor has his hands raised: he's managed to find Commander Jacoby but the policeman has a gun trained on him.

'Commander, what's going on? The Doctor's not your enemy,' you remind him.

'I wouldn't bet on that,' comments the Doctor quietly. 'The Commander here is behind the smuggling ring.'

'What? How?' you bluster.

'It's very simple,' Jacoby tells you, 'my colleagues at the Hub keep an eye out for useful bits of luggage that can become "lost", and then they mix them up with the goods to be smuggled...'

If the Doctor completes the plot, go to 59. If a new voice picks up the story, go to 51.

'But London's huge!' you gasp. 'It would take months, years, forever to find something the size of the TARDIS in London!'

'Of course it would — but not if you've got a way to trace the tiniest amount of residual Artron energy that a space/time craft gives off,' the Doctor tells you.

'Don't tell me — it's another setting on your sonic screwdriver,' you say, with an air of sarcasm. The Doctor looks a little hurt.

'It's not a magic wand, you know!' He pulls out a small crystal from his pocket which glows with a pulsating blue light. 'As this gets nearer to the TARDIS the flashes will become brighter and faster,' he explains.

The Doctor takes a look at his crystal and then sets off down the corridor.

If the signal leads you to take the lift up, go to 60. If the signal leads you to take the lift down, go to 54.

Hawkeye Pete takes a step or two closer. 'Listen,' he says to you in a conspiratorial tone, 'you look like decent people. If you scratch my back, I'll scratch yours.'

The Doctor looks at him levelly.

'What do you want?' he asks him simply.

'You're obviously looking for something and so are we. Perhaps we can help each other.'

The Doctor looks at you. 'Do you think we can trust our new friend?'

You don't look too sure and, in a nervous voice you say as much. Hawkeye's expression becomes less friendly, although his tone remains reasonable.

'I can see you two need to talk this through,' comments the pirate. 'Why don't we give you some space to do just that?'

His men take you to his ship and throw you in a cell.

If the cell is empty, go to 53. If the cell is already occupied, go to 57.

97 | The Doctor tells you that the ship has been hit by another spaceship.

'Like a car accident?' you ask.

The Doctor shakes his head. 'This wasn't an accident,' he comments, 'this was deliberate. Some idiot rammed us.'

Before you can ask the Doctor who would do something like that, you get your answer, as wildly-dressed space pirates storm into the bridge. There are a dozen or more of them, wearing eclectic clothes and brandishing a range of weapons of all ages. You see traditional cutlasses, swords and muskets as well as laser rifles and modern energy weapons.

The leader of the invaders is a scruffy-looking man with wild eyes. 'You can call me Hawkeye Pete,' he tells you, 'now hand over the StarFire or we'll tear this ship apart.'

If you get taken aboard the pirate ship, go to 72. If the Doctor thinks he knows what the StarFire is, go to 98.

'The StarFire? Wasn't that the spaceship in the revival of *Blake's Seven?*' the Doctor asks.

'Or was it a character in Marvel Comics?' you wonder.

'Imbeciles!' retorts the pirate. 'It's a fortune, that's what it is. And it's on this ship. But don't worry we'll find it.'

'Well, don't let us get in your way,' the Doctor tells him.

'I won't!' he assures you and has his men drag you back to his own spacecraft, a dirty and rundown-looking vessel that barely looks space-worthy.

Two armed pirates escort you to a cell. 'Get inside!' orders one in a guttural grunt, while the other holds the door open for you. You and the Doctor are pushed inside and then the metallic door is slammed shut.

If you've been put into an empty cell, go to 53. If the cell you are put in is occupied, go to 57.

'Welcome!' says a voice from a hidden loudspeaker. The sound is distorted, like the announcements at a train station, but there is something familiar about the voice — you feel that you've heard it before.

The Doctor is holding a small crystal that is pulsing with a purple light. 'The TARDIS is very close,' he tells you.

'Why don't you come and join me?' suggests the voice and again it is frustratingly familiar — if only you could remember where and when you have heard the voice before.

A pair of large doors slide open, revealing a cargo bay containing the TARDIS.

But before you can reach the time/space machine a figure steps out from behind it and you realise why the voice sounded familiar.

If you met 'Dave' the cleaner on the Hub, go to 24. If you met Professor Steele on the Hub, go to 44.

You wait but nothing happens. The machinery appears completely dead.

Thinking that perhaps the Doctor might arrive somewhere else on the station you exit. Directly outside the matter transporter room is a transparent-walled corridor that gives you a stunning view of the whole of the Space Station that you have arrived on. StarBase Gamma is massive, like an artificial planet. Huge skyscrapers like gantries reach out to the stars in every direction.

It is almost impossible to take in the scale of the place. Large interstellar spaceships are no bigger than insects from the distance you are looking at them. You wonder how you will ever find the Doctor.

Suddenly there is an electronic buzz from the transporter room and you run back towards it.

If you followed the Doctor into the police matter transporter, go to 88. If you went first into the police matter transporter, go to 2.

The pirate leader fires his weapon but nothing seems to happen. He pulls his trigger again and again but the gun just refuses to work.

'Sorry about that,' the Doctor tells him, with a cheeky grin, 'we don't allow weapons in here.'

Taking advantage of the pirate's confusion, Nikesh, the customs officer, lays him low with an old-fashioned punch.

'The ancient human sport of boxing,' he states proudly, 'wonderfully low-tech.'

The crisis over, the Doctor takes Nikesh back to his office.

'I'll assemble a strike force and we'll get them all arrested,' Nikesh promises.

A little while later it is time for you to say your goodbyes, then you and the Doctor are alone again.

'Home now, I think,' the Doctor announces.

You can't help but look a bit disappointed. The Doctor grins.

'But we don't have to go the direct route!' he adds.

Your adventure is over — for now.

102 The pirate leader pulls the trigger of his weapon but nothing happens. He fires again but still with no effect.

'State of Temporal Grace,' explains the Doctor with a grin, 'weapons don't work in here.'

While Hawkeye Pete is still looking at his now useless gun in amazement, Commander Steele steps forward and delivers a quick martial arts blow to the pirate's neck and he falls to the floor unconscious.

'But Venusian Aikido does,' adds Commander Steele.

The Doctor takes the Commander back to his office to organise a strike squad to take the remaining pirates into custody and soon you and the Doctor are alone again in the TARDIS.

'Now where?' you ask.

The Doctor sets some controls.

'Now I really should get you back to twenty-first century Earth,' he announces. He looks up and sees your expression. 'But not right away, eh?'

Your adventure is over — for now.

Step into a world of wonder and mystery with Sarah Jane and her gang in:

1. Invasion of the Bane
2. Revenge of the Slitheen
3. Eye of the Gorgon
4. Warriors of the Kudlak

And don't miss these other exciting adventures with the Doctor!

1. The Spaceship Graveyard
2. Alien Arena
3. The Time Crocodile
4. The Corinthian Project
5. The Crystal Snare
6. War of the Robots
7. Dark Planet
8. The Haunted Wagon Train
9. Lost Luggage
10. Second Skin
11. The Dragon King
12. The Horror of Howling Hill